The Tomten

A PaperStar Book, published in 1997 by Penguin Putnam Books for
Young Readers, 345 Hudson Street, New York, NY 10014.
PaperStar Books is a registered trademark of The Putnam Berkley Group, Inc.
The PaperStar logo is a trademark of The Putnam Berkley Group, Inc.
Originally published in 1961 by G. P. Putnam's Sons.
Published simultaneously in Canada.
Manufactured in China
L.C. Number: 61-10658
ISBN 0-698-11591-0
9   10   8

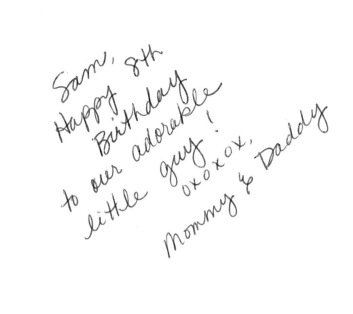

Sam, 8th
Happy
Birthday
to our adorable
little guy!
oxoxox,
Mommy & Daddy

The Tomten

ADAPTED BY ASTRID LINDGREN FROM A POEM BY VIKTOR RYDBERG

ILLUSTRATED BY HARALD WIBERG

Penguin Putnam Books for Young Readers

It is the dead of night. The old farm lies fast asleep and everyone inside the house is sleeping too.

The farm is deep in the middle of the forest. Once upon a time someone came here, cut down trees, built a homestead and farmed the land. No one knows who. The stars are shining in the sky tonight, the snow lies white all around, the frost is cruel. On such a night people creep into their small houses, wrap themselves up and bank the fire on the hearth

Here is a lonely old farm where everyone is sleeping. All but one...

The Tomten is awake. He lives in a corner of the hayloft and comes out at night when human beings are asleep. He is an old, old tomten who has seen the snow of many hundreds of winters. No one knows when he came to the farm. No one has ever seen him, but they know he is there. Sometimes when they wake up they see the prints of his feet in the snow. But no one has seen the Tomten.

On small silent feet the Tomten moves about in the moonlight. He peeps into cowshed and stable, storehouse and toolshed. He goes between the buildings making tracks in the snow.

The Tomten goes first to the cowshed. The cows are dreaming that summer is here, and they are grazing in the fields. The Tomten talks to them in tomten language, a silent little language the cows can understand.

"Winters come and winters go,

Summers come and summers go,

Soon you can graze in the fields."

The moon is shining into the stable. There stands Dobbin, thinking. Perhaps he remembers a clover field, where he trotted around last summer. The Tomten talks to him in tomten language, a silent little language a horse can understand.

> *"Winters come and winters go,*
>
> *Summers come and summers go,*
>
> *Soon you will be in your clover field."*

Now all the sheep and lambs are sleeping soundly. But they bleat softly when the Tomten peeps in at the door. He talks to them in tomten language, a silent little language the sheep can understand.

"All my sheep, all my lambs,

The night is cold, but your wool is warm,

And you have aspen leaves to eat."

Then on small silent feet the Tomten goes to the chicken house, and the chickens cluck contentedly when he comes. He talks to them in tomten language, a silent little language chickens can understand. "Lay me an egg, my jolly chickens, and I will give you corn to eat."

The dog kennel roof is white with snow, and inside is Caro. Every night he waits for the moment when the Tomten will come. The Tomten is his friend, and he talks to Caro in tomten language, a silent little language a dog can understand.

"Caro, my friend, is it cold tonight? Are you cold in your kennel? I'll fetch more straw and then you can sleep."

The house where the people live is silent. They are sleeping through the winter night without knowing that the Tomten is there.

"*Winters come and winters go,*

I have seen people large and small

But never have they seen me," thinks the Tomten.

He tiptoes across to the children's cot, and stands looking for a long time.

"If they would only wake up, then I could talk to them in tomten language, a silent little language children can understand. But children sleep at night."

And away goes the Tomten on his little feet. In the morning the children see his tracks, a line of tiny footprints in the snow.

Then the Tomten goes back to his cozy little corner in the hayloft. There, in the hay, the cat is waiting for him, for she wants milk. The Tomten talks to the cat in tomten language, a silent little language a cat can understand.

"Of course you may stay with me, and of course I will give you milk," says the Tomten.

Winter is long and dark and cold, and sometimes the Tomten dreams of summer.

>"*Winters come and winters go,*
>
>*Summers come and summers go,*
>
>*Soon the swallows will be here,*" thinks the Tomten.

But the snow still lies in deep drifts around the old farm in the forest. The stars shine in the sky, it is biting cold. On such a night people creep into their small houses and bank the fire on the hearth.

Here is a lonely old farm, where everyone is fast asleep. All but one...

Winters come and summers go, year follows year, but as long as people live at the old farm in the forest, every night the Tomten will trip around between the houses on his small silent feet.